Waltham Forest Libraries

Please return this item by the last date stamped. The loan may be renewed unless required by another customer.

MAY 19		
		D1513669

Need to renew your books?
http://www.walthamforest.gov.uk/libraries or
Dial 0333 370 4700 for Callpoint – our 24/7 automated telephone renewal line. You will need your library card number and your PIN. If you do not know your PIN, contact your local library.

Enid Blyton

A WISHING-CHAIR
ADVENTURE

OFF ON A
HOLIDAY ADVENTURE

For Flyn and Calissa
A. P.

EGMONT
We bring stories to life

Cover and interior illustrations by Alex Paterson

Text first published in Great Britain as chapters 7-8
of *The Wishing-Chair Again*, 1950
Published as *Off on a Holiday Adventure: A Wishing-Chair Adventure*, 2019
by Egmont UK Limited
The Yellow Building, 1 Nicholas Road, London W11 4AN

Enid Blyton ®, The Magic Faraway Tree ®
and Enid Blyton's signature are registered trade marks of
Hodder & Stoughton Limited
Text © 1950 Hodder & Stoughton Limited
Illustrations © 2019 Hodder & Stoughton Limited

ISBN 978 1 4052 9267 2

www.egmont.co.uk

A CIP catalogue record for this title is available from the British Library

Printed in Malaysia

68896/001

Enid Blyton

A WISHING-CHAIR
ADVENTURE

OFF ON A
HOLIDAY ADVENTURE

EGMONT

CHAPTER ONE
OFF ON A HOLIDAY ADVENTURE

For a whole week the children watched and waited for the wishing-chair to grow its wings again. It didn't sprout them at all! The wings had vanished as soon as it had arrived safely back in the playroom.

'I hope its magic isn't getting less,' said Mollie, one day, as they sat in the playroom, playing ludo together. It was their very **favourite game**, and they always laughed at Binky because he made such a fuss when he didn't get 'home' before they did.

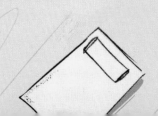

As they sat playing together they felt a welcome draught. 'Oh, **lovely!** A breeze at last!' said Mollie thankfully. 'I do really think this is just about the hottest day we've had these holidays!'

'The wind must have got up a bit at last,' said Peter. 'Blow, wind, blow – you are making us lovely and cool.'

'Funny that the leaves on the trees aren't moving, isn't it?' said Binky.

Mollie looked out of the open door at the trees in the garden. They were **perfectly still!** 'But there *isn't* a breeze,' she said, and then a sudden thought struck her. She looked round at the wishing-chair, which was standing just behind them.

Look!' she cried. 'How silly we are! It isn't the wind – it's the wishing-chair that has grown its **wings** again. They are flapping like anything!'

So they were. The children and Binky sprang up in delight. 'Good! We could just do with a **lovely cool ride** up in the air today,' said Peter. 'Wishing-chair, we are very pleased with you!'

The wishing-chair flapped its wings very strongly again and gave a **creak**. Then Binky noticed something. 'I say, look – it's only grown *three* wings instead of four. What's happened? It's never done that before.'

They all stared at the chair. One of its front legs hadn't grown a wing. It looked rather **odd** without it.

Binky looked at the chair rather doubtfully. 'Do you think it can fly with only three wings?' he said. 'This is rather a **peculiar** thing to happen, really. I wonder if we ought to fly off in the chair if it's only got three wings instead of four.'

'I don't see why not,' said Mollie. 'After all, an aeroplane can fly with three engines, if the fourth one stops.'

The chair gave a little **hop** up in the air as if to say it could fly perfectly well. 'Oh, come along!' said Binky. 'We'll try. I'm sure it will be all right. But I wish I knew what to do to get the fourth wing to grow. Something has gone wrong, it's plain.'

They got into the chair, Binky as usual sitting on the back, holding on to their shoulders. The chair flew to the door.

CHAPTER TWO
HIGH UP IN THE AIR

'Where shall we go?' said Binky.

'Well – we never did get to the Land of Goodness Knows Where after all,' said Mollie. 'Shall we try to get there again? We know it's a good way away, so it should be a nice long flight, very cool and **windy** high up in the air.'

'We may as well,' said Binky. 'Fly to the Land of Goodness Knows Where, chair. We saw it on the map – it's due east from here, straight towards where the sun rises – you go over the **Tiptop Mountains**, past the **Crazy Valley** and then down by the **Zigzag Coast**.'

'It sounds exciting,' said Mollie. 'Oh, isn't it lovely to be cool again? It's so very hot today.'

They were now high up in the air, and a lovely breeze blew past them as they flew. Little clouds, like **puffs** of cotton wool, floated below them. Mollie leaned out to get hold of one as they **passed**.

'This is fun,' she said. 'Binky, is there a **land of ice-creams?** If so, I'd like to go there sometime!'

'I don't know. I've never heard of one,' said Binky. 'There's a Land of Goodies though, I know that. It once came to the top of the Faraway Tree, and I went there. It was lovely – biscuits growing on trees, and chocolates sprouting on bushes.'

'Oh – did you see Moon-Face and Silky and the old Saucepan Man?' asked Mollie, in excitement. 'I've read the books about the Faraway Tree, and I've always wished I could climb it.'

'Yes, I saw them all,' said Binky. 'Silky is **sweet**, you'd love her. But Moon-Face was cross because somebody had taken all his slippery-slip cushions – you know, the cushions he keeps in his room at the top of the tree for people to sit on when they **slide** down from the top to the bottom.'

'I wouldn't mind going to the Land of Goodies at all,' said Peter. 'It sounds really fine. I almost **wish** we'd told the chair to go there instead of the Land of Goodness Knows Where.'

'Well, don't change its mind for it,' said Binky. 'It doesn't like that. Look, there are the Tip-Top Mountains.' They all leaned out to look. They were very extraordinary mountains, running up into high, jagged peaks as if somebody had drawn them **higgledy-piggledy** with a pencil, up and down, up and down.

On they went, through a batch of tiny little clouds; but Mollie didn't try to catch any of these because, just in time, she saw that **baby elves** were fast asleep on them, one to each cloud.

'They make good cradles for a hot day like this,' explained Binky.

After a while, Mollie noticed that Binky was leaning rather hard on her shoulder, and that Peter seemed to be leaning against her, too. She pushed them back.

'Don't lean so **heavily** on me,' she said.

'We don't mean to,' said Peter. 'But I seem to be leaning that way all the time! I do try not to.'

'Why are we, I wonder?' said Binky. Then he gave a cry. 'Why, the chair's all on one side. No wonder Peter and I keep going over on to you, Mollie. Look – it's **tipped sideways!**'

'What's the matter with it?' said Mollie. She tried to shake the chair upright by swinging herself about in it, but it always over-balanced to the left side as soon as she had stopped swinging it to and fro.

They all looked in **alarm** at one another as the chair began to tip more and more to one side. It was very difficult to sit in it when it tipped like that.

'It's because it's only got three wings!' said Binky, suddenly. 'Of course that's it! The one wing on this side is **tired out**, and so the chair is flying with only two wings really, and it's tipping over. It will soon be on its side in the air!'

'Gracious! Then for goodness' sake let's go down to the ground at once,' said Mollie, in alarm. 'We shall fall out if we don't.'

'Go down to the ground, chair,' commanded Peter, feeling the chair going over to one side even more. He looked over the side. The one wing there had already **stopped flapping**. The chair was using only two wings – they would soon be tired out, too!

CHAPTER THREE
A SPELL FOR GROWING WINGS

The chair flew heavily down to the ground and landed with rather a **bump**. Its wings stopped flapping and hung limp. It creaked dolefully. It was quite exhausted, that was plain!

'We shouldn't have flown off on it when it only had three wings,' said Binky. 'It was wrong of us. After all, Peter and Mollie, you have grown bigger since last holidays, and must be **heavier**. The chair can't possibly take us all unless it has *four* wings to fly with.'

They stood and looked at the poor, tired wishing-chair.'What are we going to do about it?' said Peter.

'Well – we must try to find out where we are first,' said Binky, looking round. 'And then we must ask if there is a **witch** or **wizard** or magician anywhere about that can give us something to make the chair grow another wing. Then we'd better take it straight home for a rest.'

'**Look**,' said Mollie, pointing to a nearby sign-post. 'It says, "To the Village of Slipperies". Do you know that village, Binky?'

DAME QUICK FINGERS.

'No. But I've heard of it,' said Binky. 'The people there aren't very nice – **slippery as eels** – can't trust them or believe a word they say. I don't think we'll go that way.'

He went to look at the other arm of the signpost and came back looking very pleased.

'It says "Dame Quick-Fingers",' he said. 'She's my great-aunt. She'll help us all right. She'll be sure to know a spell for growing wings. She keeps a pack of **flying dogs**, you know, because of the Slipperies – they simply fly after them when they come to steal her chickens and ducks.'

'Goodness – I'd love to see some flying dogs,' said Mollie. 'Where does this aunt of yours live?'

'Just down the road, round a corner, and by a big rowan tree,' said Binky. 'She's really nice. I dare say she'd ask us to tea if we are as polite as possible. She loves **good manners**.'

'Well – you go and ask her if she knows how to grow an extra wing on our chair,' said Mollie. 'We'd better stay here with the chair, I think, in case anyone thinks of stealing

it again. We can easily bring it along to your aunt's cottage, if she's in. We won't carry it all the way there in case she's not.'

29

'Right. I'll go,' said Binky. 'I won't be long.
You just sit in the chair till I come back – and
don't you let **anyone** steal it.'

He ran off down the road and disappeared
round a corner. Mollie and Peter sat down in
the chair to wait. The chair creaked. It
sounded very tired indeed. Mollie patted its
arms. 'You'll soon be all right once you have
got a fourth wing,' she said. '**Cheer up**.'

Binky hadn't been gone very long before the sound of footsteps made the children look round. Five little people were coming along the road from the Village of Slipperies. They looked **most peculiar**.

'They must be Slipperies,' said Peter, sitting up. 'Now we must be careful they don't **play a trick** on us and get the chair away. Aren't they odd-looking?'

The five little creatures came up and bowed low. '**Good-day**,' they said. 'We come to greet you and to ask you to visit our village.'

CHAPTER FOUR
THE SLIPPERIES PLAY A TRICK!

Peter and Mollie looked hard at the five Slipperies. Each Slippery had one **blue** eye and one **green**, and not one of them looked straight at the children! Their hair was slick and smooth, their mouths **smiled without stopping**, and they rubbed their bony hands together all the time.

35

'I'm sorry,' said Peter, 'but we don't want to leave our chair. We're waiting here with it till our friend Binky comes back from seeing his Great-Aunt Quick-Fingers.'

'Oh, she's **gone to market**,' said one of the Slipperies. 'She always goes on Thursdays.'

'Oh dear,' said Peter. 'How tiresome! Now we shan't be able to get a fourth wing for our wishing-chair.'

'Dear me – is this a wishing-chair?' said the Slipperies, in **great interest**. 'It's the first time we've seen one. Do let us sit in it.'

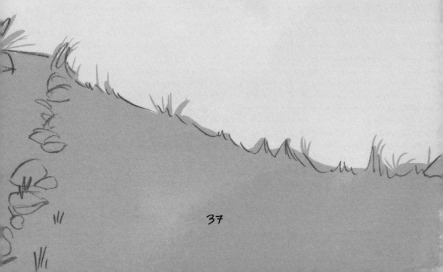

'Certainly not,' said Peter, feeling certain that if he let them sit in the chair they would try to fly off in it.

'I hear that Great-Aunt Quick-Fingers has some flying dogs,' said Mollie, hoping that the Slipperies would look frightened at the mention of them. But they didn't. They rubbed their slippery hands together again and went on smiling.

'Ah, yes – **wonderful dogs** they are. If you stand up on your chair, and look over the field yonder, you may see some of them flying around,' said one Slippery.

The children stood on the seat of the chair. The Slipperies clustered round them. 'Now look right down over that field,' began one of them. 'Do you see a tall tree?'

'Yes,' said Mollie.

'Well, look to the right of it and you'll see the roof of a house. And then to the right of that and you'll see another tree,' said the Slippery.

'Can't you tell me **exactly** where to look?' said Mollie, getting impatient. 'I can't see a single flying dog. Only a rook or two.'

'Well, now look to the left and . . .' began another Slippery, when Peter jumped down from the chair.

'You're just making it all up,' he said. 'Go on, **be off with you!** I don't like any of you.'

The Slipperies lost their smiles, and looked nasty. They laid hands on the wishing-chair.

'I shall **whistle** for the flying dogs,' said Peter suddenly. 'Now let me see – what is the whistle, ah, yes . . .' And he suddenly whistled a very shrill whistle indeed.

The Slipperies shot off at once as if a
hundred of the flying dogs were after them!

Mollie laughed.

'Peter! That's not really a whistle for flying
dogs, is it?'

'No, of course not. But I had to get rid of
them somehow,' said Peter. 'I had a feeling
they were going to **trick us** with their silly
smiles and rubbing hands and odd eyes – so
I had to think of some way of tricking them
instead.'

'I wish Binky would come,' said Mollie,
sitting down in the chair again. 'He's been
ages. And it's all a waste of time, his going to
find his Great-Aunt, if she's at the market.

We shall have to go there, I expect, and carry the chair all the way.'

'Why, there is Binky!' said Peter, waving. 'Oh, good, he's dancing and smiling. He's got the spell to make **another wing grow**.'

'Then his Great-Aunt couldn't have gone to market!' said Mollie. 'Hey, Binky! Have you got the spell? Was your Great-Aunt Quick-Fingers in?'

'Yes – and awfully pleased to see me,' said Binky, running up. 'And she gave me just enough magic to make another wing grow, so we shan't be long now.'

'**Five** Slipperies came up, and they said your Great-Aunt always goes to market on Thursdays,' said Mollie.

'You can't believe a word they say,' said Binky. 'I told you that. My word, I'm glad they didn't trick you in any way. They usually trick everyone, no matter how clever they may be.'

'Well, they didn't trick us,' said Peter. 'We were **much too smart** for them – weren't we, Mollie?'

'Yes. They wanted to sit in the chair when they knew it was a wishing-chair,' said Mollie. 'But we wouldn't let them.'

'I should think not,' said Binky. He showed the children a little blue box. 'Look – I've got a smear of ointment here that is **just enough** to grow a red wing to match the other wings. Then the chair will be quite all right.'

'Well, let's rub it on,' said Peter. Binky knelt down by the chair – and then he gave a **cry** of horror.

'What's the matter?' said the children.

'Look – somebody has cut off the other three wings of the chair!' groaned Binky. 'Cut them right off short. There's only a stump left of each.'

Mollie and Peter stared in horror.

CHAPTER FIVE
THE POOR, TIRED WISHING-CHAIR

Sure enough the other three wings had been cut right off. But how? And when? Who could have done it? The children had been with the chair the whole time.

'I do think you might have kept a better guard on the chair,' said Binky **crossly**. 'I really do. Didn't I warn you about the ways of the Slipperies? Didn't I say you couldn't trust them? Didn't I . . .'

'Oh, Binky – but when could it have been done?' cried Mollie. 'I tell you, we were here the **whole of the time**.'

'Standing by the chair?' asked Binky. 'Yes – or on it,' said Peter.

'On it! Whatever did you stand on it, for?' said Binky, puzzled. 'To stop the Slipperies sitting down?'

'No – to see your Great-Aunt's flying-dogs,' said Peter. 'The Slipperies said they were over there, and if we would stand up on the chair seat we could just see them **flying around**. But we couldn't.'

'Of course you couldn't,' said Binky. 'And for a very good reason, too – they're all at the cottage with my Great-Aunt. I saw them!'

'Oh – the dreadful **story-tellers!**' cried Mollie. 'Peter – it was a trick! Whilst we were standing up there trying to see the dogs, one of the Slipperies must have quietly snipped off the three wings and put them in his pocket.'

'Of course!' said Binky. 'Very simple – and you're a pair of simpletons to get taken in by such a **silly trick**.'

Mollie and Peter went very red. 'What shall we do?' asked Peter. 'I'm very sorry about it. Poor old chair – one wing not grown and the other three snipped away. It's a shame.'

'Thank goodness Binky has the Growing Ointment for wings,' said Mollie.

'Yes – but I've only got just enough for one wing,' said Binky. 'One wing isn't going to take us very far, is it?'

'No,' said Mollie. 'Whatever are we going to do?'

'I shall have to ask Great-Aunt Quick-Fingers for some more Growing Ointment, that's all,' said Binky, **gloomily**. 'And this time you can come with me, and bring the chair too. If I leave you here alone with it, you'll get tricked again, and I shall come back and find the legs are gone next time, and I can't even grow wings on them!'

'It's not nice of you to keep on and on about it, Binky,' said Mollie, lifting up the chair with Peter. 'We're very sorry. We didn't

know quite how clever the Slipperies were.
Oooh – horrid creatures, with their odd eyes
and deceitful smiles.'

CHAPTER SIX

GREAT AUNT QUICK FINGERS

They followed Binky down the road and along a lane. Soon he came to his Great-Aunt's cottage. It was very snug and small. To Mollie's **enormous delight**, five or six little brown dogs, rather like spaniels were flying about the garden on small white wings. They barked loudly and flew to the three of them.

'Now, now – these are friends of mine,' said Binky, and patted the nearest dog, which was flying round his head.

It was strange to have the little dogs **sailing** about the air like gulls! One flew up to Mollie and rested its front paws on her shoulder. She laughed, and the dog licked her face. Then off it flew again, and chased after a sparrow, barking madly.

Great-Aunt Quick-Fingers came to the door, looking surprised. 'Why, Binky – back again so soon!' she said. 'What's happened?'

Binky told her. 'So you see, Great-Aunt, now that the **poor chair** has lost all its wings, I'm afraid that the Growing Ointment you gave me won't be enough,' said Binky. 'I'm so sorry.'

'Well, well – it takes a very clever person to see through the Slippery ways,' said his Great-Aunt. 'You'd better come in and have tea now you're all here!'

The children put down the wishing-chair and Great-Aunt Quick-Fingers got the little **treacle tarts** out of the oven. 'There you are,' she said. 'Get your fingers nice and sticky with those! I'll go and make some more Growing Ointment for you. It won't take long.'

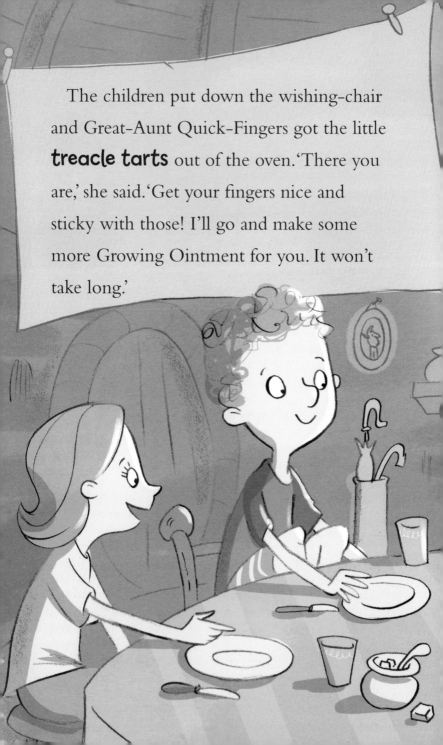

She disappeared, and the children sat and munched the lovely treacle tarts.

Just at that moment she came back, with a fairly large jar. She handed it to Binky. 'There you are. Use that and see what happens. **But remember**, you can only use it once on anything. The spell doesn't act twice. It's no good trying to use the ointment another time on the chair, to make it grow wings, because it won't be any use.'

Binky dipped his finger into the jar of ointment. It was curious stuff, bright yellow with green streaks in it.

He rubbed some on to a chair leg and immediately a **most wonderful wing** sprouted out, big and strong!

'I say – it isn't red, as it always is!' cried Mollie. 'It's green and yellow – and a much bigger wing than before. I say, chair, you will look grand. Make another wing come, Binky.'

Soon the wishing-chair had four grand
green and yellow wings, much bigger than
its old red ones. It waved them about proudly.

'You'd better get in the chair and go before
it tries its new wings out by itself,' said Great-
Aunt Quick-Fingers. So in they all got, Binky
on the back, as usual – and off they went!

'Home, chair, home!' cried everyone, and it rose high in the air, and flew off to the west. 'Goodbye and **thank you very much**,' cried Binky and the children, and Great-Aunt waved till they were out of sight.

66

'Well, that was quite a nice little adventure,'
said Peter. 'And the chair's got some **wonderful**
new wings. I do hope they'll always grow like
this in future – big and strong, and all green
and yellow!

The FARAWAY TREE Adventures

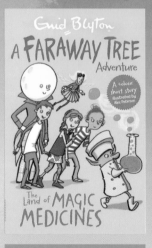

Enid Blyton
A FARAWAY TREE
Adventure
A colour short story illustrated by Alex Paterson
The Land of BIRTHDAYS

Enid Blyton
A FARAWAY TREE
Adventure
A colour short story illustrated by Alex Paterson
The Land of MAGIC MEDICINES

Enid Blyton
A FARAWAY TREE
Adventure
A colour short story illustrated by Alex Paterson
The Land of DO-AS-YOU-PLEASE

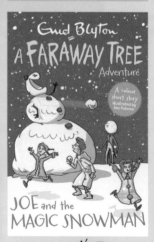

Enid Blyton
A FARAWAY TREE
Adventure
A colour short story illustrated by Alex Paterson
JOE and the MAGIC SNOWMAN

Enid Blyton
A FARAWAY TREE
Adventure
A colour short story illustrated by Alex Paterson
The Land of TOYS

Enid Blyton
A FARAWAY TREE
Adventure
A colour short story illustrated by Alex Paterson
The Land of ENCHANTMENT

Collect all the magical
FARAWAY TREE Adventures – packed full
of exciting new colour illustrations!

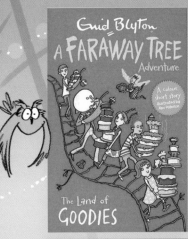